I0818306

for laughing and maturing on the journey,
Elias, Ada & Joanna

scratches & scribbles: R. J Dyson
edits & whatnot: Brooke Dyson

Galaxy picture from Pixabay. Real nice.
The character image of Grape was designed by E. J. Dyson.

First Printing: 2017
ISBN 978-0-9914581-8-9
Absolutely Unprofessional
Wadsworth, OH 44281

absolutelyunprofessional.com

The Oddventures of

DOUGHNUTS, DUNGAREES & DISCIPLES

absolutelyunprofessional

WELCOME
to
WIDDLEWORTHINGTONVILLE

Home

PROSPECT St.

CORKS
&
Bobbers
GENERAL Store

NAKED
Knife
SHOP

HIGH St.

BOYER St.

the
balcony

SHADEE'S INS.

MAPLE St.

Police
Station

COFFEE &
DOUGHNUTS

WORM
HOLE

GAZEBO

HOLE

COLLEGE St.

SECRET DOOR

SONNET'S
BONNETS

MAIN St.

Clock
TOWER

MILLS St.

It's me again, Bartus. We need to talk about my fainting spells - so embarrassing. Journal, do you realize just how chancy capes are? And that giant grapes are super friendly? I'd watch out for onions, though. Onions are fierce.

Anyhoo, on our way to fetch a doughnut and a fresh pair of dungarees yesterday, Toe Jam, the young dude I'm discipling, finally said his first encouraging word.

So awesome!

It was a big day for a big dude.
Or dog?
Rabid hamster?
Atomic kitty?

Whatever he is, he's pretty radnacious.

In fact, I'd say he's matured by heaps and lumps on this spiritual adventure by my side. I'm honored that's he willing to learn from me.

My pupil.

My intern.

My young **disciple**.

Yesterday was a good day. Let's see if I can write it all down before I forget. That's right, the day began nice and early...

9:31 A.M.

Jumping from our third story attic window I hit the Kentucky bluegrass with a tuck n' roll.

'Front door still works,' said Toe Jam, strolling down the steps.

Crossing Prospect St. I saw Dargon the super-awesome, red-cape wearing delivery man arrive on schedule. Dargon is totally DUTEOUS.

'See that, Toe Jam? Heart of a servant in full effect.' I'm not so sure Toe Jam collected the same golden nuggets of wisdom from Dargon's actions.

Super-dude gave me a thumbs up!

DUTEOUS: dew-tea-yus
Dutiful, obedient.
Like me, just doing what I'm told from womb
to tomb. Hold the whipcream!
Didn't Bartus say something about Jesus' call
to obedience as a disciple?
Or was that a call to obesity? Dang.

Dargon's rad.

9:47 A.M.

That's when Weird Beard the, uh, average dog flew by wearing a tube sock. No, tube socks aren't shirts, but Weird Beard sure looks dignified in that thing.

'How about you, Toe Jam? Do you wear confidence like a tube sock?'

'I wear confidence like a speedo,' he said.

'Yikes. **U.G.I.**' I said. '**U**nnecessary **G**raphic **I**magery.'

9:59 A.M.

'How's it fluffin' Sava the Flava? What a bear, what a bear.
Man he can really groove.
I like a good groove.
I like a good jam.
Apricot jam.
Apricot jam on my hand in the sand!'

'I heard that!' said Sava.

'Not even planned.'

'I heard it, but I don't get it,' groaned Toe Jam.

We're just spittin' a bit. Sava's teaching me to let the rhymes run.

'Hmmm. Like when you plant the Word deep inside your soul until it overflows in tidal waves of grace and truth as the Spirit leads?' said Toe Jam, the budding sage.

'Exactly! Dude, what a fantastic analogy.' It's safe to say I was totally shocked.

'I want avacado ice cream,' Toe Jam said.

It sure can take time to see spiritual fruit in the life of a new disciple. Toe Jam, for instance, is a lot like an avacado tree. Why? Because an avacado tree takes about five years to produce delicious avacados. And even more delicious guacamole, baby!

While I'm still not sure what species he is, I think he said he's only five in our human years but 30 in his mammalian creature years. That little dude really is like an avacado tree - ready to bear fruit any day now.

'Umm... Seriously, Bartus. Ice cream. Mouth. Now.'

He's one crazy-awesome apprentice.

SIDE-NOTE TO MYSELF:

Remind Toe Jam about Paul's letter to that ancient church in Corinth (1 Corinthians 11:1). Sure he's not Jewish, Greek, Mayan or Jamaican, I really have no clue what he is, but he can totally grab the same rhythm of life as that Super-Disciple, Paul.

10:11 A.M.

No one will ever believe what happened next. Especially Aunt Cantankerous. She's way too disagreeable. But, I suppose there's always hope.

Anyway, before we passed **THE NAKED KNIFE SHOP** on High St., I saw it shimmering like a smattering of strawberry jelly on the brick wall. There she stood, Pizza Prudence the Pedestrian. Just an everyday giant pizza leaning on the back alley dumpster and staring into the middle distance with crispy-wide pepperoni eyes.

Sauce was everywhere!

Golden brown crust sliced up all sad and delicious-like. Black olives strewn about. Tomato chunks at my feet. She even had some advice for me.

Never haggle with a knife salesman. Never!
DUMP

Some great advice for sure, but I wasn't all that interested in buying knives at the moment.

'Prudence, I'd hate to leave you like this. Can we grab a few sandwich baggies, some napkins, a to-go box and buzz a taxi for you?' I asked.

'No thanks, Bartus. I've got it under control.'

Prudence, that lively slice o' back alley pizza, never entered a knife shop without a plan. Full of hope and spunk. Spunk and moxy. Spoxy faith baby!

What a sweet slice of awesomeness.

Whoa, my stomach's gurgling... Is that strange or do you get the munchies when she's around, too?

10:28 A.M.

Seriously, that evil demon-lizard will drink up the joy in your soul like a slushie through a curly-straw.

10:30 A.M.

We turned left at CORKS AND BOBBERS GENERAL STORE when the sun disappeared. Seemed a bit odd for 10:30am, especially as a gale blew down from above (Toe Jam rudely blamed me as he stood down wind). That's when Cap'n and The Neil appeared sailing through the watermelon sky.

'The Neil, would you swab the poop deck, dear?' asked the Cap'n. 'Reeks of a keister's brouhaha!'

'Well now, anything for the bravest she-Cap'n in the land. Ain't nothin' but a joy to clean up after them loose-bowelled Belly Whompers!'

Even after all these years I'm not really sure what Cap'n and The Neil do. Or what a Belly Whomper is. Though, I did hear some local **chitty-chitty-chat-chatty-chit-chat** about a black and white rainbow over a giant kitty cat constellation ending on an island of misfit blue-blob piddlers.

Whatever they do, their CORDIALITY is totally infectious. What an awesome husband and wife duo!

Someday I'm gonna get hitched to a fine young lady like that there Cap'n.

CORDIAL: kor-jul
Heartfelt, warm and friendly.
Pretty much sums *me* up. That's right,
Cordial is my third middle name:
Charles Philbert Cragney Cordial
Toe Jam Gustoferson III.

10:41 A.M.

And of course there's Dargon again. Super delivery dude delivering super goods to super strange, cape-wearing people in town.

Dedication to obligation.

Love it!

Keeping notes little dude?

Get off my extremely cute and furry little back, Bartus.

Toe Jam wasn't interested in notetaking at the moment. Thankfully he's learning to shift grumpy-gears sooner than later.

'I'm sorry. Those cow pies for breakfast aren't settling well,' he said. 'Should've eaten 'em weeks ago!'

Quick to listen, slow to speak and even slower to get angry, young grasshopper.

10:53 A.M.

Babycakes, Babycakes,
oh my little hover-quakes.

If you're thinking there isn't anything to learn from a handful of miniature floating birthday cakes singing sultry songs about scrumptious edibles down on Boyer St...

You'd be wrong.

Always on the cusp of being Sava the Flava's SACCHARIFEROUS after supper sweets, these floating Babycakes remain as **sans souci** as a puppy in a **cream puff pastry**. Yeah, that's right, I said *sans souci*.

'Toe Jam, it's time to call **Master Takeshi**, martial arts extraordinaire.'

'What's he got to do with those creepy, floating, singing baby birthday cakes?' asked Toe Jam.

'Are you kidding? We need protection from their killer vocal chops!'

'Master Takeshi couldn't chop a carrot with a double-edged sword.'

'There's no need to be snarky, little puppy-dude,' I said. 'Let's take it easy on the retired samurai.'

'Besides, I have a better plan to avoid their seditiously sugared songs. I'll be over here stuffing my ears with gravel,' he grouched. 'And my eye, too.'

Toe Jam is an incredibly creative INSULTINATOR. I can't wait until he uses his verbal gymnastics to encourage others instead.

'Oh, and my teeth, too. Lot's of teeth rocks should help crunch out the soul depleting sounds of Babycakes.'

SACCHARIFEROUS:
sack-a-rih-fur-us
Containing or producing sugar.
A sweet trick-or-treat for my
rotund seat! Hmm, puppy-pastry sounds
good, too....

11:07 A.M.

Do you know what happened next, journal?

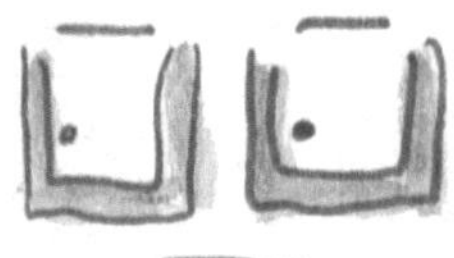

Of course you don't. You're just a bound wad of shaved up tree. Better than being a tissue, right? Actually, tissue's are pretty vital too!

So let me tell you how my heart did floateth unto the heavens just after 11:07.

'Hello my little Bartus-Boo!' said Penelope Pennington, batting her easter-egg eyes and singing out from her second story bedroom balcony on Boyer St.

With the very confidence of a tube sock wearing winged-wiener dog, my mouth sprung wide and began to squeal in awkward-operatic-spurts:

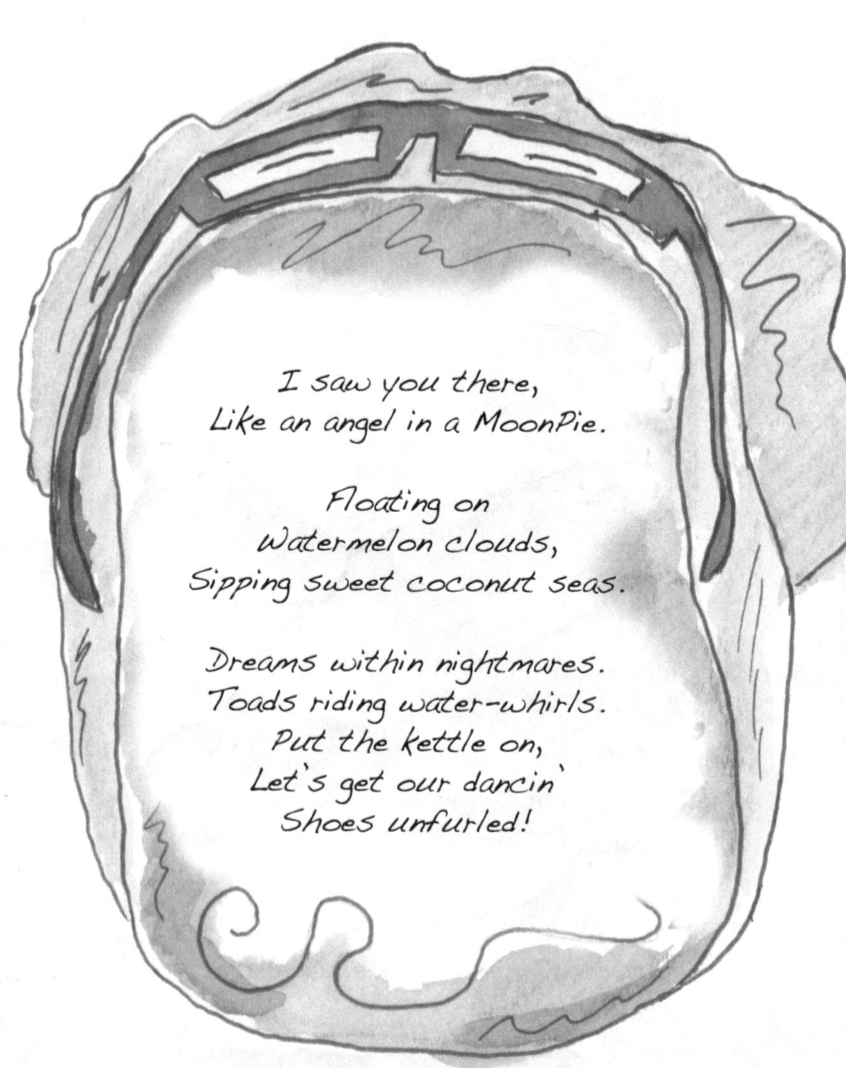
I saw you there,
Like an angel in a MoonPie.

Floating on
Watermelon clouds,
Sipping sweet coconut seas.

Dreams within nightmares.
Toads riding water-whirls.
Put the kettle on,
Let's get our dancin'
Shoes unfurled!

Trees stretched out their arms in unison.

Rocks belted out in baritone bellows.

Clouds stared down with jolly eyes.

Dargon appeared crowing along like an alleycat under a mystical moonlit southern sky.

Catching my breath I turned around with cheeks as fiery red as a **baboon's buttocks**. That's when I saw the true reason for Penelope's easter-egg eyes. The supreme mathemagician, spelling bee superstar and stunning Scripture scholar - *Bartus-Boo Incrediblue* towering over me. That's right, there's another Bartus in town. One year older. One foot taller. And totally awesome.

Apparently I'm no Boo.

'Wow, did you hear that? Pretty sure that was the endlessly reverberating echo of embarrassment,' said Toe Jam.

The world began to spin as a thick fog rolled in. In fact, details are still a bit hazy on that whole opera charade. Oddly, I don't have any problem recalling Toe Jam's clever comments afterward.

Toe Jam hasn't quite grasped the artful craft of silence in certain scenarios. A little grace goes a long way.

MORTIFIED: More-tih-fyed
To be embarrassed, ashamed
or humiliated.
In other words, Bartus' childhood. Ha!
Awww, now I feel bad.

'Your cheeks kinda look like two of those 99 red balloons,' said Toe Jam. 'Ya know, from that German band. Dancy tune man, dancy.'

'There's something wrong with you.'

11:10 A.M.

Obviously I had to immediately resume my journey toward doughnuts and dungarees. So I bailed on Boyer and hung a right down Maple St. Passing the police station I was forced to an abrupt halt by the incredible Officer Agent.

'Young man, you have the rosy-glow of a **baboon's buttocks**. Are you feeling alright today?' He actually said that.

Seriously, there's got to be a better red-cheeked analogy than a primate's caboose.

'Nothing more than bruised pride,' I said.

'Hmm. So that was your operatic ditty moments ago, eh?' Officer Agent said with a kindly smirk. So awesome.

Sometimes it's just better to own the embarrassment.

'He's taking requests, too, officer!' said Toe Jam.

Note to Self: Investigate the legal ramifications of caging an inhuman talking Toe Jam.

ANOTHER NOTE TO THIS SELF:
Don't actually cage the obnoxious little pseudo-cat.
Forgive man. Just forgive. I need to go and read
Matt 6:14-15 again, and maybe
a little taste of
Ephesians 4:31-32.

11:15 A.M.

Skipping down Maple St. we stumbled into a parallel dimension.

Again.

There I was staring back at myself. 'Polkadots? Sweet bow tie!' I was totally excited to learn all about the rad life of an alternate Bartus Mathetes. So, I asked my other self the first question that popped into my mind...

Then my alternate me asked the first question that came to his mind.

Word travels fast!

He even had a few unkind words for Toe Jam.

'And what's with that soulless varmint? Smells like a dead cow and moves like a dying blobfish out o' water,' said parallel-Bartus. Sheesh, my omni-dimensional me was snarky.

The INSULTINATOR followed with his own verbal revenge.

Mr. Omni-dimensional Bartus - You, sir, emit an offensive pong. As though a spraying zorilla threw-up a rotten egg into a blooming corpse flower!

'Turn the other cheek, little buddy,' I said.

'He called me a blobfish! Have you seen a blobfish?'

'Listen, if someone ruffles your Toe Jammin pride, ignore it. Even when they do it again and again.'

'And pass up a hand-crafted comeback like that?' he whined.

'You'll never regret it. Anyhow, it seemed a little odd that there wasn't an omni-dimensional version of you,Toe Jam?' I said.

'Well, that was your alternate dimension, not mine,' the furry little disciple replied.

'Is that really how alternate dimensions work?'

'I don't wanna get into the hairy, spine-bending details on multiple dimensions today,' he said, calm as a koala. 'Like Gammy always said, humans just don't have the brain capacity to understand the dimensional depths of this perfectly designed universe.'

If nothing else, that alternately-bitter-me was proof that a Bartus isn't always better on the other side.

'Besides,' said Toe Jam, 'my Gammy say's I'm way too cute to replicate a bajillion times over in infinitely alternate dimensions. My cutenacity would explode a million suns and a billion hearts.'

'No doubt. So what's with the skivvies? And you're kinda freaking me out with that crossed eye and slobber deal?'

'Uh swallowed uh haew,' mumbled Toe Jam.

'You swallowed a hair? Well, your Royal Cuteness, I agree that we're better off with one Toe Jam in our own universe.'

That was that. When we finally returned to our own neighborhood we discovered that time had leapt forward several hours.

Crazy timewarp stuff!

4:47 P.M.

Back on High St. I was shocked to see Dargon again.

'What in the cow pasture is going on around here? Dargon, you really get around super dude.' It's a bit freaky, actually. He's like, everywhere. Either that or warping to another dimension messed with our own time / space continuum.

That's when it happened. Dargon spilled a box full of red capes into the street.

'Need a hand, super dude?'

That's when I saw the steam roller carelessly careening down the road. Dargon, however, was totally unaware. How could he not see it lurching forward?

Dargon, look out super awesome delivery dude!

Toe Jam, what can we do?

Please tell me you're not licking that nasty old brick wall again?

Like a wallaby hopping into an old-fashioned cowboy tuck n' roll, Dargon cleared the path of the 20 ton behemoth at the last moment. Seven thumbs up all around!

Unfortunately, his own red cape stuck to a gooey piece of cherry gum on the giant steel roller.

'Oh. Eww. Ouch. Look at that. I'll never eat sausage again,' said Toe Jam. 'Oh look, here comes a street sweeper. How appropriate.'

'Dargon met his end as an astonishing model of awesomeness. Wouldn't you agree, Toe Jam?'

'Mmm... skunk's been here.'

'So unnecessary.'

And so ended **Dargon**, the super awesome, kind-hearted supporting character.

5:01 P.M.

Seriously, that evil demon-cat will scrape the kindness off of your bones like frosting from a mixing bowl. Hiding dragons, crouching ligers, what's up with my small town… *Sheesh!*

5:03 P.M.

There she was, Volcanna Sugar, scaling the wall of SHADEE'S INSURANCE CO. on High St. She, too, saw the demise of Dargon.

'Can you believe it, fellas?' she cried out, flipping through the air like a squirrel on a sugar high. 'I'll never get to hear another long-winded tale of red-caped heroics.'

'No more Dargon-jargon,' said Toe Jam.

'I sure am gonna miss him,' she said, tears in her costume covered eyes. 'You boys may wanna hightail it. I can't contain my heartache much longer.'

'Nah, I'm more of a low-tail kinda guy,' said Toe Jam.

'Do you remember the second stage of discipleship, Toe Jam?' I find it's always a good idea to capture the moment for a life lesson.

'Ummm... You teach and I eat a bag of cheesy-poofs?'

'Close, good buddy. But that's the first stage,' I said. 'And take a break from licking that wall for a moment.'

'You're running out of time!' yelled Volcanna.

'Nailed it! Mental notes, nice job.' I was impressed. He's a bit of a blank paper some days so it's hard to know when he's learning and when he's, well, licking an old brick wall.

'So, stage two is when I serve beside you, a prematurely balding college guy who knows Jesus,' he said.

My Discipler!

Mentor!

Instructor?

Go home!

'Sounds like we're all on the same page. Love in action, mon frere,' I said.

'Got it. But what does this little lesson in disicplmaking have to do with the exploding superhero lady telling us to run?'

'Volcanna? Great question! Good students ask questions, well done Toe Jam.' High pressure scenarios squeeze the pulp out of our minds. 'In this instance, follow closely as I...'

'Why are we running?' huffed Toe Jam.

'Well, she isn't called Volcanna for nothing. When that super-redhead gets upset she makes Mt. Vesuvius look like a ladybug-toot. Lava showers, my strange little friend. Lava showers!'

When someone signals **pain** and **suffering**, take heed.

STAGES OF DISCIPLESHIP

Stage 1: Discipler does the teaching and training. I do the eating of cheesy-poofs.

Stage 2: Discipler invites me to serve alongside him. Only if it's a soft-serve, ya know, that chocolate & vanilla swirl? *Delicious!*

Stage 3: Now I initiate the serving and learning and my discipler supports me. Like when I'm grilling a squirrel for the neighbors, my discipler brushes on the worcestershire sauce!

Stage 4: I'm now inviting others into the disciple-making journey while my discipler supports me from the couch eating cheesy-poofs.

Actually, those are my cheesy poofs. Get your own dang POOFS!

:as taught by **Toe Jam**
Stage 1
Keep On
Keepin' On
Begin
Here
Stages
of
Disciplemaking
Stage 2
Stage 4
Stage 3

Go on now...
Get your own
dang POOFS!

5:25 P.M.

Turning down College St. Toe Jam ran into Mayor Wild-Dove. Literally. Nearly took her out at the shins.

'Aaagghhhh, sorry Miss Mayor,' said Toe Jam, rubbing his cranium.

Hello gentlemen. Great to see you around town, Commodore Awesome and co.

Yeah, that's just a special nickname they gave me around town. Last year I wrote a formal letter to the mayor's office asking to be called **Commodore Awesomepants**.
Oddly, they agreed! But on the singular condition that they would leave the *'pants'* behind. For sure, I mean, who needs pants? So, it's official, I'm Commadore Awesome!

‘Want the usual today, Mayor Wild-Dove?’ As wildly protective of her town as a mama bear, yet as peace-loving as a morning dove.

What a fantastic mayor!

‘One medium black coffee will do just fine, gentlemen. Oh, and don’t forget a splash of 2% milk and two sugars, stirred to perfection.’

‘Commodore Awesome and the ever present Toe Jam, ready for service.’

So, we added a coffee detour to our doughnut and dungaree mission. Anything for the mayor.

NOTE TO OLD SELFY-SELF:

Have Toe Jam read Paul's note to disciples in the city of Galatia (Galatians 6:9-10). There's something about being a servant to others, even if it's just grabbing a coffee, that fosters awesome spiritual maturity through all stages of life.

5:33 P.M.

THE REDEMPTIVE SAGA OF FANCY-FIGHTIN' FINBAR

Fancy-Fightin' Finbar marched down the deep-dark-alley.

Stout and strong as a Shetland pony with hair as wild as a maple tree ablaze. Bed-Head was a small town force to be reckoned with.

With each step from beyond the alley Fancy-Fightin' Finbar shook the ground. The biggest bully this side of the MISSISSIPPI BULLY MUSEUTORIUM.

'Listen, Fancy Finbar, we don't want to cause any trouble,' I said.

'Yeah, Fat-Head Fartley, we're just lookin' for doughnuts, dungarees and a medium black coffee with a splash of 2% milk and two sugars, stirred to perfection,' Toe Jam chimed in. 'So back off, pony-boy!'

'The overflow of your heart, little dude. Let's not assume our stout and stodgy neighbor is here to put the hurt on.'

That's when buildings began to violently shake as a blast of crayon-melting hot air blew in.

Without warning the sidewalk cracked open delivering all three of us into an abyss. Toe Jam and I, screaming like pre-schoolers with chocolate puddin' cups, held tight to one another as Fancy-Fightin' Finbar bounced off craggy walls and broken city pipes.

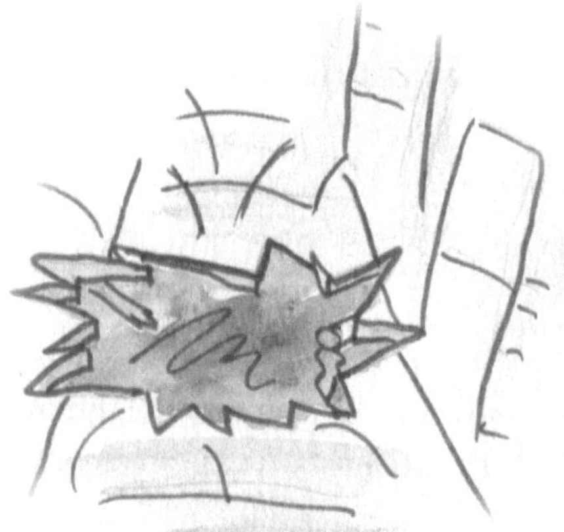

Landing in a pile of legs and limbs, we untangled to find an abandoned subterranean city.

Or so it appeared.

'Wow… I always wondered about this place,' said Fancy Finbar.

'You mean, you've heard of these ancient catacombs?' I asked.

'These were my people,' he said, tears piling up on his rosy cheeks. 'I've searched for kin since I was knee-high-to-a-potbelly-pig.'

Turns out that Fancy-Fightin' Finbar wasn't the only Shetland pony-sized character in our little town. Long before I was a twinkle in my pappy's eye, his tribe provided most of the county with wicked-potent cow manure.

'Back in the day ya'll turned on us! Ya'll said our manure stank. That families were suffocating in the fog of our splendid stench. So they hunted us down with clothes pins on their snouts throwing potpourri bombs at us!'

'Potpouri bombs, now that ain't right!' said Fightin' Finbar.

'Dude, I had no idea. But why did you stay behind?' I was hooked. Fancy Finbar sure tells a good backstory.

'Is that why you're such a big-headed stinky rascal?' asked Toe Jam. Not an emotional creature.

'I'm not a rascal! I'm disgruntled. Wouldn't you be if your entire tribe had been driven away by local grocers swinging hunga-mungas? Then left behind by your family in the fray!'

Fancy-Fightin' Finbar released the waterworks.

A salty, sloshy, muddy sort of slobbering.

He cried so much that the subterranean streets began to flood.

I guess some more slushy slobbering happened.
A little over-the-top if you ask me. Literally over my head.

So, Toe Jam and I did what anyone would do, we jumped aboard an old wooden pastry cart, grabbed some giant bread dough paddles, and pulled Fancy-Fightin' Finbar from the inglorious deluge.

'Something's moving up ahead!' I said.

Sure enough, a herd of wild-haired, stout-bodied, Shetland-sized humanoids emerged from the ruins. Fancy-Fightin' Finbar snapped to attention.

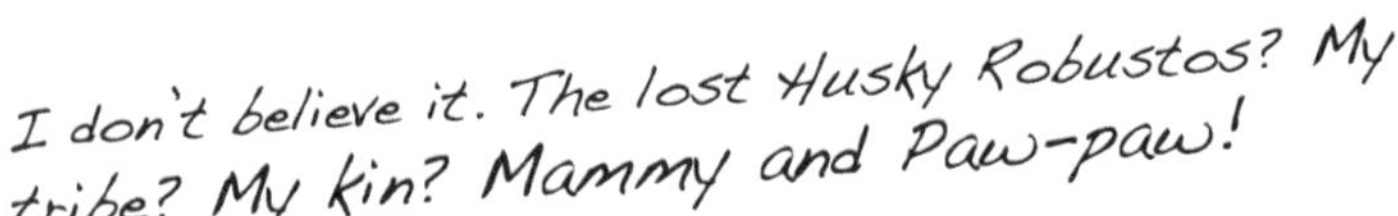

With all of Fancy Finbar's blubbering and all the stumbling and stomping of the Robusto Tribe, the waves in the caves swished and swashed. Dizzied by the great chaos, Toe Jam and I lost control of our pastry barge. From one side of that great subterranean hall to the other we spun wildly out of control.

Undeterred, we managed to rescue a hefty Husky Robusto with each pass. Within minutes we recovered that whole mangy lot with our makeshift rescue vessel.

'Dramamine...' Toe Jam moaned. 'I ain't got my sea legs, cap'n!'

'Hold your gully, little buddy. We'll be on solid ground soon enough.'

As the water continued to rise, the Shetland-sized tribe joined in the waterworks. 'Tell 'em to quit their blabbering,' said Toe Jam.

'**NO!!!**' I shouted. 'Keep the floodgates open. We've only got one shot at this. Once the water reaches the ceiling, as long as we're directly beneath the hole in the sidewalk, the pressure will spit us out like a loogie from the spout of a whale!'

That's when the Husky Robustos began to sing in unison. Fancy-Fightin' Finbar took the lead as a smooth tenor. I'm still not sure where they found the instruments.

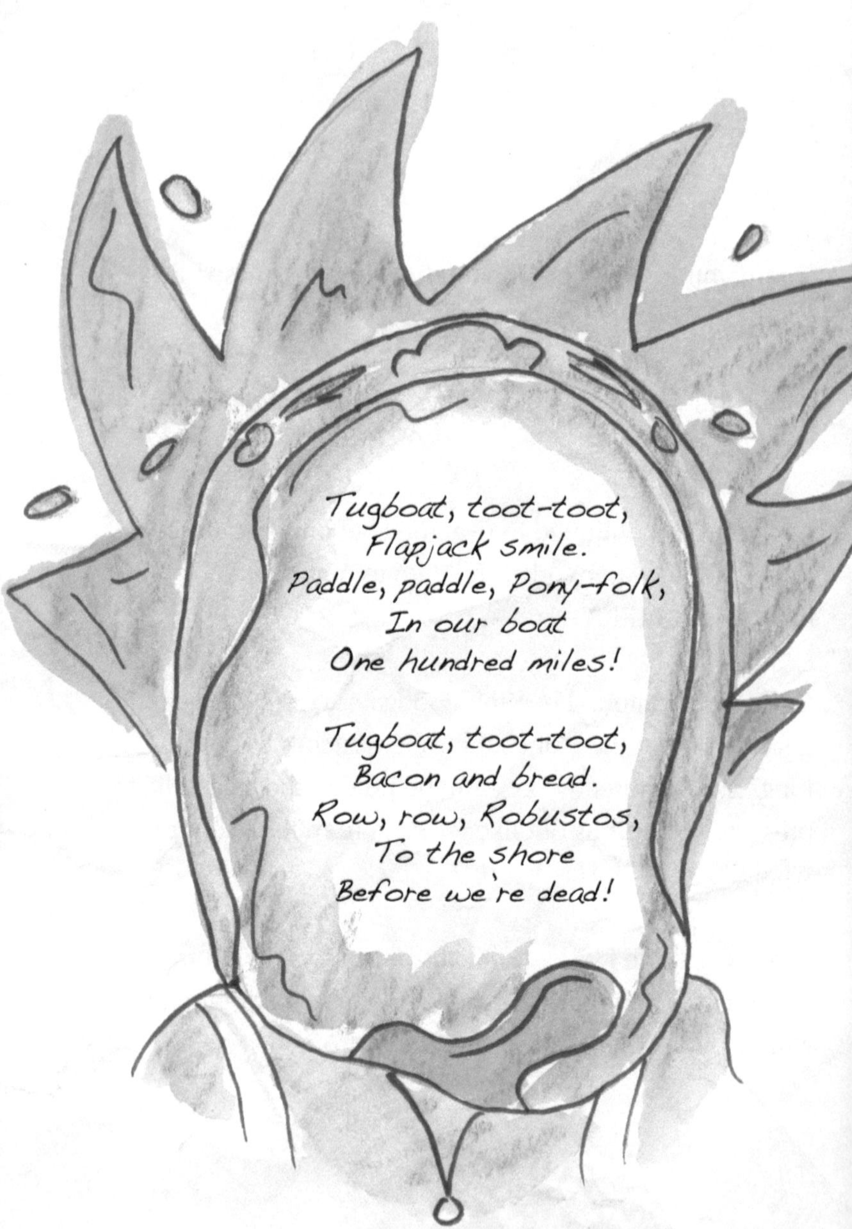
Tugboat, toot-toot,
Flapjack smile.
Paddle, paddle, Pony-folk,
In our boat
One hundred miles!

Tugboat, toot-toot,
Bacon and bread.
Row, row, Robustos,
To the shore
Before we're dead!

Before we knew it, Toe Jam, myself, Fancy-Fightin' Finbar and the gnarly lot of Husky Robustos were all safely above ground.

'Thank you, Bartus,' said Fancy Finbar. 'And you as well little doggy. I suppose you'll be on your way to fresh doughnuts, some dungarees and a cup of black coffee with milk and sugar.'

'Stirred to perfection...' said Toe Jam, wildly tossing his brunch in the corner.

Dozens of hugs and handshakes later, with some of the sweetest and smelliest manure-scented mortals we'd ever met, Toe Jam and I hit the pavement.

'So, young cadet, any new insight on your opinion of Fancy-Fightin' Finbar?' I asked.

'Blubbering pony-boy?' said Toe Jam. 'Maybe one thing I guess. Seems that hurt people seem to hurt people.'

Crazy, the same creature that just threw up a tire spoke with gut-dropping spiritual profundity. 'So then, how might that discovery help all disciples first respond to loud-mouths like Fightin' Finbar?'

'Honestly, I'd rather ignore that Shetland-sized oaf... but that card you gave me with the memory verse on it said something about making peace. Or was it pizza? Is today pizza day?' said Toe Jam. 'Make pizza, not war!'

'Respond with cautious but courageous peace-filled words and deeds,' I said. 'Be diligent in being a peacemaker.'

'Pacemaker? Does manure-boy have heart problems?'

'Sacrificing your own safety to rescue strangers and offer peace is a sure sign that you're living the way of Christ,' I said. 'You did great back there, Toe Jam. Now go mop up your gnarly upchuck.'

6:21 P.M.

You know what, Bartus?
I'd love to clean up my
mess...

But I CAN do the shuffle!

And a headstand...

And the inchworm...

I call this the Levitating Hairball!

Yikes! My eviltwin!

Look Ma, I'm
all out invisible.

Done yet?

For sure.
I'll grab a
mop.

7:00 P.M.

We skipped down Watrusa Ave. and you wouldn't believe who we ran into next. That's right, the red-cape wearing, spandex-bodysuit-sporting, Dargon.

Dargon? How the... your cape... steam roller?

Toe Jam gracefully followed my sputtering lead. 'Spandex dude? You were totally squished like a ketchup packet!'

'Classy, Toe Jam,' I said. 'Sometimes observations ought to be muted, not blabbed.'

An honorable servant never leaves a job undone.

'So true, super spandex-bodysuit cape-guy.' Journal, I'm not sure if he's an ultra model of dedication OR the ultimate workaholic. Either way, it's good to see him.

That super-guy's undisputedly STUPEFYING.

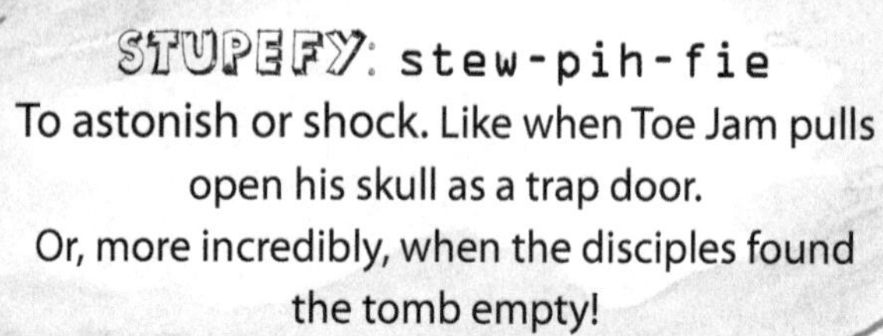
STUPEFY: stew-pih-fie
To astonish or shock. Like when Toe Jam pulls open his skull as a trap door.
Or, more incredibly, when the disciples found the tomb empty!

7:10 P.M.

Once again, Dargon soared off to fulfill his spandex dreams. Toe Jam and I, however, stumbled to a much needed rest behind SONNET'S BONNETS.

This bench is CRUSHING my spine.
That's because it's not a bench... it's a broken cinder block.
Oh.

Toe Jam's observation skills leave something to be desired. On the other hand, he's quite exceptional with flavors.

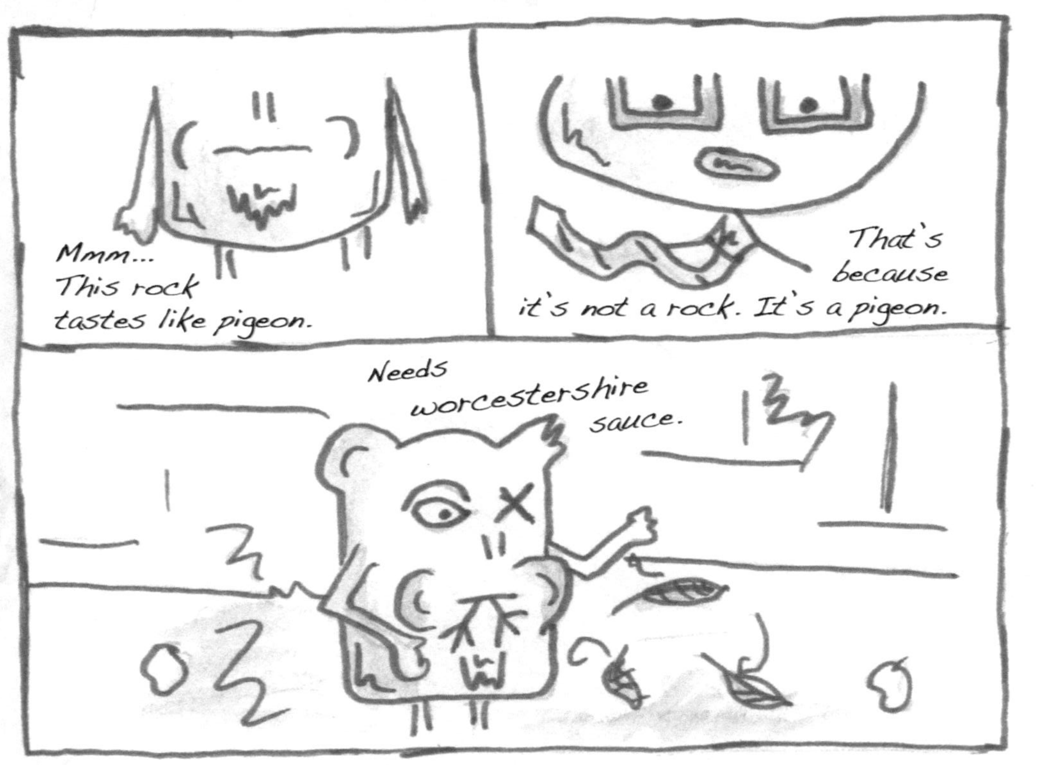
Mmm...
This rock
tastes like pigeon.
That's
because
it's not a rock. It's a pigeon.
Needs
worcestershire
sauce.

...and maybe some
basswood honey.

7:14 P.M.

We turned left on Mills heading for Main St.

Mayor Wild-Dove was anticipating one medium black coffee with a splash of 2% milk and two sugars, stirred to perfection. A handshake, a head nod and our word as men *(man and fuzzy creature)* we held to our mission like angry bees on a clueless squirrel.

Not to mention our own doughnuts and dungarees.

'Uh, Bartus?'

'What's up, Toe Jam? And what's with the bonnet?'

'Found it in the dumpster. Ya know how you and I have that thing to get to tonight?'

'Sure do. It's super important. Might even shape the rest of my life.'

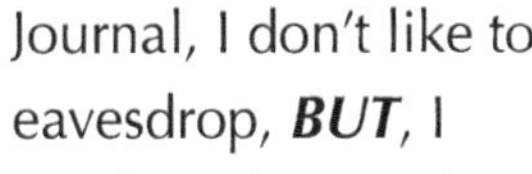

Journal, I don't like to eavesdrop, ***BUT***, I overheard mom chitty-chat-natter-prattling with Uncle Biscuit over the phone three days ago and the event pretty much sounds historic in scope and scale.

And journal, I don't usually build a case on scuttlebutt, ***BUT***, Uncle Biscuit hired a professional sign company to wrap his car with an advertisement which read:

IT'S GOING TO BE THE BIGGEST NIGHT OF HIS LIFE!

Still, I thought they were being a tinsy-bit dramatic until I received a letter from the president. Not **POTUS**, but the president of CHARLEY O' HOOLIHAN'S DOG FOOD CO. Turns out he's one of Uncle Biscuit's closest friends and really wanted to share a few encouraging words before the big day. Real nice.

Anyhow, according to that giant clock over there, we have seven minutes 'til showtime.

Bartus? You alright? Seven minutes man!
Did you just pass out?
MMMMMMM... an old pan of burnt bacon.

7:16 P.M.

A moment later Grape roused me with a refreshing splash of orange juice.

7:17 P.M.

Another minute passed and Grape was able to stir me to full attention.

'Now get ahold of yourself, Commodore Awesomepants,' said the giant not-raisin. And yes, it's worth noting that he added '**pants**' to the end of my self-ordained title.

Definitely the coolest grape on the vine.

‘While you were a pile of passed-out flesh, Toe Jam tweeted your conundrum. He’s got you covered, dude.’

‘Toe Jam tweets?’

‘Listen to this enlivening exhortation in less than 140 characters:

'Pretty sweet. I hear he's one of your DISCIPLES. Keep tending, mon frere. Keep tending,' said Grape.

'Yeah, for sure.'

'You're dedication is paying off Commadore. I mean, check me out! It wasn't too long after you trained up Pepperoni Prudence that she took my sister and I under her saucy slice as young students,' said the giant fruit, ripe with gratitude.

'Right on, Grape. That's how Master Yeshua set it in motion. We make disciples who go along making disciples.' As for Toe Jam, I had hope that one day after years

and years

and years

and years

and years

and years

and years of modelling and training and encouraging, that he would live his own honorable life. Turns out that day began to dawn yesterday. Radness!

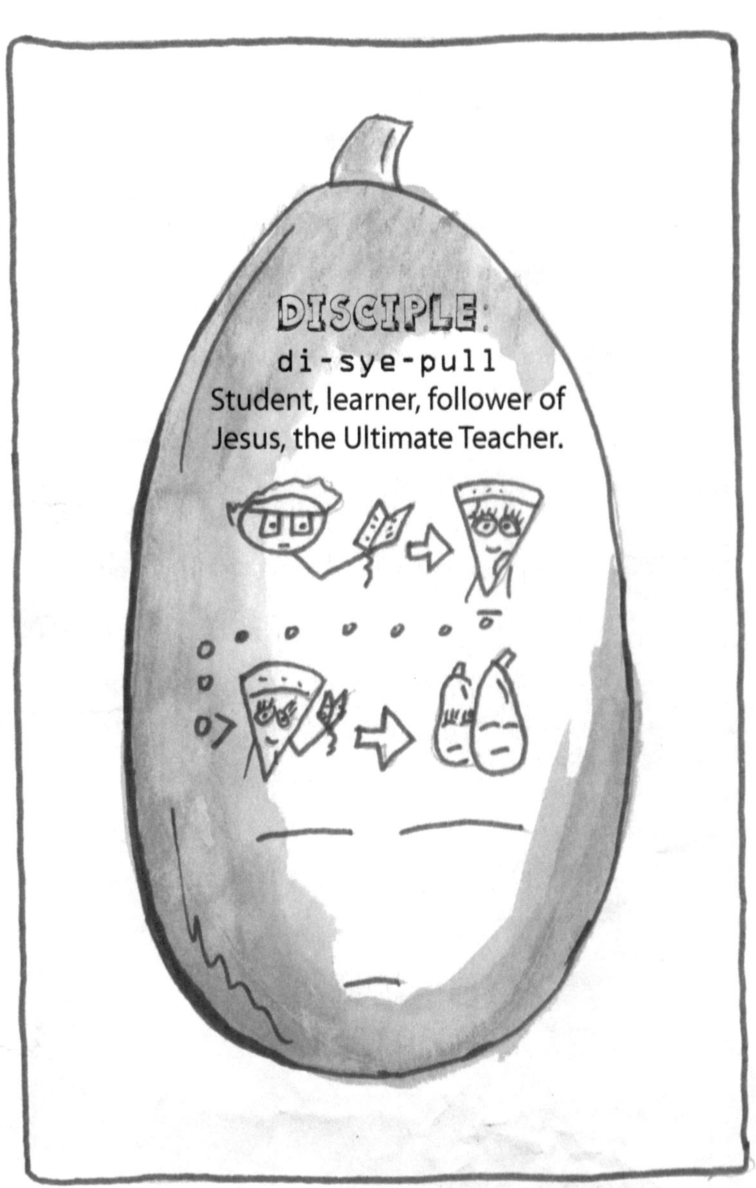
DISCIPLE:
di-sye-pull
Student, learner, follower of
Jesus, the Ultimate Teacher.

'Are those tears?'

'They sure are, Grape. Salty, yet ever so sweet,' I said wiping my eyes. 'Now give me the rundown.'

'Here's where we stand: Toe Jam's off fetching doughnuts, I'm waiting on the seamstress, the crowd's forming, and Volcana's attempting to obtain one medium black coffee with 2% milk and two sugars, stirred to perfection.'

'Whoa! You really are an amazing fruit-of-the-vine my huge purple friend not named Barney,' I said.

'I hear the coffee's for Mayor Wild-Dove,' said Grape.

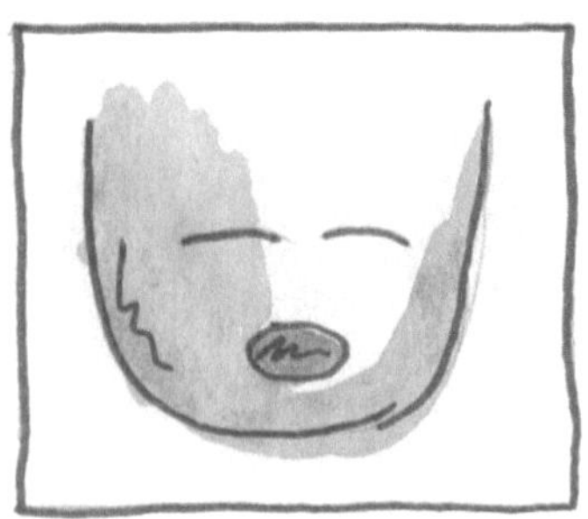

She's Phenomenal!

She's Dynamiticus!

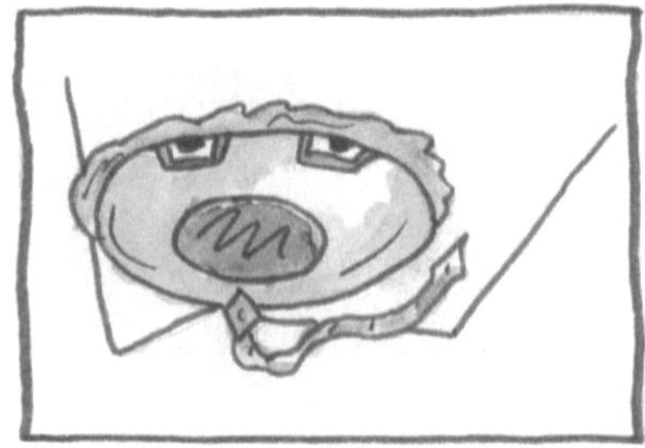

Fabulacious Sensatious!

The Magnificent Mayor from Widdleworthingtonville!

I'd follow her into a Brown Recluse infested inferno of icky idolatrous Bramble Bashers!

'No, no, no, Grape. Dungarees! Three minutes to go and I've still got to find some dungarees to wear.'

'Of course you do my brotha from anotha species,' said Grape. 'That's why I'm waiting on a seamstress.'

'Seamstress?'

'Fancy-Fightin' Finbar and a strout tribe of Husky Robustos answered the tweet offering a new pair of hand-stitched dungarees,' said Grape. 'Speak o' the Shetland-sized tribe, here comes the seamstress now.'

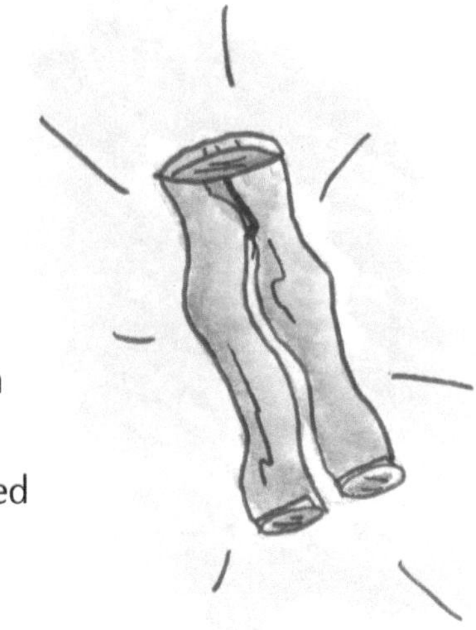

'Are those dungarees spun out of gold?' I asked in awe. The stout tribe nodded with pleasure.

'Sure are, Commodore Goldenpants.' Grape winked and I knew he meant it. 'Two minutes to spare you big-hearted Bartus you. Best get to gettin' while the gettin's good.'

Heavenly music washed over us as Babycakes provided a soundtrack of inspiration and instigation. And maybe a little indigestion. Seriously though, nothing better than hovering birthday cakes in chorus as we race to the end of our mission.

Love me some a capella!

To be honest, I was still in awe of Toe Jam's burst of servanthood. Talk about acting on the *one-anothers*.

Egg morphing into larva.

Disciple maturing into teacher.

What a remarkable little creature.

A CAPPELLA: ah kah-pelluh
Singing without instrumental
accompaniment.
Wait, without a band? *Lame*.

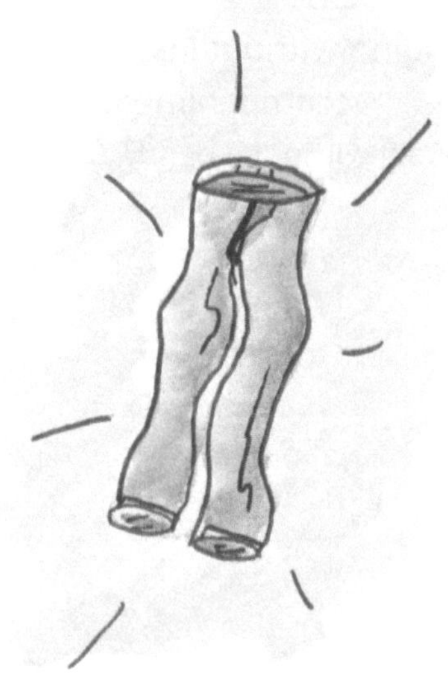

Hey journal, check out my pantaloons.
Wink - wink, click - click.
Wink - click - blink.
Click - wink - wink.
Click - click - blink.
Click - wink.
Real nice.

7:19 P.M.

Having slipped into my handstitched dashing golden dungarees, it was time to follow in the footsteps of wiser disciples than I… and pray.

Pretty sure it was Nehemiah, an ancient king's cupbearer-turned-leader, who modelled the shotgun prayer.

Light as a ladybug, quick as a goat! Lord, turn my tipsy-toes into swift deer hoofs with rubber tread. Make me quick as a buck!

And King David prayed for just about everything imaginable, even for hoofs like a deer. If there's anyone to copy in a moment of need then old King David's not a bad choice.

Feeling spry I turned to race onward and the scene before me was stunning. Widdleworthingtonville had responded to Toe Jam's tweet in full force.

Sava the Flava was there with granny.

Still looking fancy-free at age 153!

My allergenic yurt-dwelling neighbors showed up for a raucous round of optimistic-banner-waving.

So collaboratively colorful. **Totally awesome!**

Don't forget to rest you asthmatic charismatics!

And of course the floating Babycakes' were belting it out just as Volcanna Sugar burst through the crowd with the mayor's hot coffee. Stirred to perfection and ready for a sip.

Thanks Volcanna! You super-stealthy, lava-bubble of coffee-clutching heroine awesomeness.

And who would've guessed that even the weirdos from TABLE NUMBER NINE (the ultimate downtown diner) would find their way into the gauntlet of admiration.

Cap'n and The Neil were on the sidelines with their herd of loose-bowelled Belly Whompers. Yes, they were letting loose their bowels like miniature blue whales, flocculent and flatulent.

Cautious yet Kind,
Prudence. Well done!

There she was in the crowd, confidently standing beside the salesman from THE KNIFE SHOP. A new friend for a new day.

Mayor Wild-Dove stepped forward like an olympian waiting for the baton. Without spilling a drop she took hold of the delivery.

Mission: Wild-Dove-Medium-Black-Coffee-Delivery: Check.

Weird Beard the flying dog was there, too. And honestly, who doesn't like a compliment?

Yep, there she was, Penelope Pennington. And who was standing by her side? None other than Bartus-Boo, the super theologica-mathemagician wearing really sweet aviators.

Right on!

Hoards of onlookers filled the square as the final seconds ticked by.

'Grab the bear! Slap the pig! Eat the cheese! Stop the clock!' I yelled in a fit.

'What's the problem little man?' said Grape, inexplicably beside me.

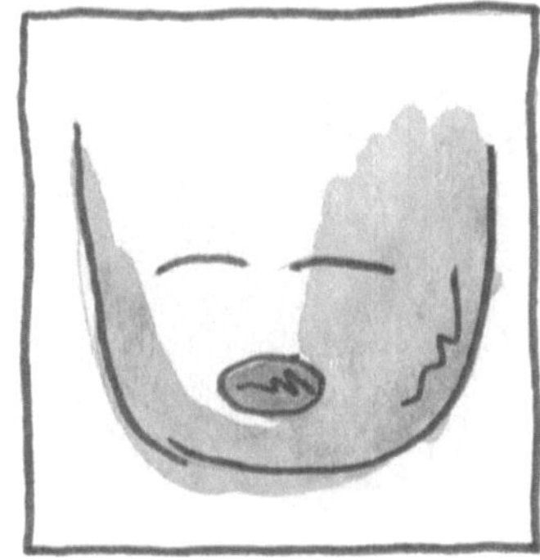

'I can't possibly complete the mission without my sidekick. My student. Toe Jam!'

7:21 P.M.

Then came that familiar scratchy voice. Of course my Aunt Cantankerous wouldn't believe what happened next, but I know you will, journal.

You're really stepping it up today, Toe Jam. But since when do you wear a cape? Are you flying?

Thank you - Since now - Yes - And it's just a little chicky-birdie snacky-poo.

With a pint-sized thud, Toe Jam descended. Side by side we entered the gazebo.

With Grape to my left and Toe Jam to my right, that awesome cape-wearing Dargon kicked off our super special night.

'Dargonnit! I'm so excited, and I just can't hide it!' said Dargon with an uncomfortably drawn-out laugh before diving into his super-prepared speil for the super-awesome event.

Commodore Awesomepants, right along with your grodious and odious furry little sidekick with a ripening heart, I, Dargon the Beefy, on behalf of our incredible town of Widdleworthingtonville hereby bestow upon you the...

Crowds cheered.

Uncle Biscuit forcefully winked. 'Whoa, Uncle B. Don't hurt yourself!' His heart isn't as sour as his face.

'This is one heavy key... quite colossal! Toe Jam, check it out!' I offered.

With an open mouth and an empty stomach the key disappeared.

MmMMmmm...
What I wouldn't give
to wash it down with a
tunafish smoothie!

The crowd **gasped.**

Dargon **wheezed.**

I **snortled.**

Mayor Wild-Dove laughed. A hearty laugh, too. Like a giant cannibal chicken choking on a turkey leg.

Best. Laugh. Ever.

With the crowd in a frenzy over the gobbled-up key, she leaned in and with a hushed voice said, 'Only the true of heart, mind, body and soul may possess the KEY TO WIDDLEWORTHINGTONVILLE. You're a true servant, Bartus, and your disciple's actions today validate your genuine faith.'

'But he's eaten it,' Grape interjected.

'He's eaten a lot today and like the rest... this too shall pass,' said Mayor Wild-Dove with an exceptional wink.

So patient and so wise.

'One request though...' said the mayor, her eyes piercing my gully. 'When you discover the key's hidden secrets, and I have no doubt you will, drop by my office.'

'Sounds mysteriously ominous,' I whispered.

'Intrigued?' asked Mayor Wild-Dove.

'Yes, of course, well, you see…'

'Spit it out, Commodore,' she said, sipping her black coffee with a splash of 2% milk and two sugars, stirred to perfection.

'Well, the key fits in that giant wooden door with the silver lock,' I said, pointing to a giant wooden door with a silver lock across High Street in an abandoned alley.

'Leads to an old silver mine,' said Toe Jam. 'I used to play there as a wee little dirt-urchin. All sorts of time-portals, anti-gravity mine-fields and wormholes. My cousin Gart, looks like a pickled-blobfish, is still stuck in some radioactive chamber of commerce or some old mess of a place. Fun stuff. Wanna see? I keep an old picture of a solar family party under my tongue.'

Activities for the whole Jam fam!

One surprise after another with this discipleс.

ANOTHER NOTE TO ME:

The mayor's right - I need to remember to tell Toe Jam that we don't make ourselves pure or sinless, instead, when we love Jesus with our heart, soul, mind and strength He reveals His mysteries to us. Be sure to study Mark 12:28-34 with him. Real nice!

7:35 P.M.

The stroll home was joyfully uneventful.

Cars whirred by in a haze of cheers. Toe Jam rocked *It's a Long Way to the Top (If You Wanna Rock 'N' Roll)* on air guitar. And I mean he really destroyed that thing. I think he smashed it over the trunk of an apple tree in the encore.

It was a good day.

7:41 P.M.

Back in the attic things were quiet.

'I almost forgot,' said Toe Jam emerging from the restroom with some pastries in his paws, 'I snagged two doughnuts on my way to the gazebo. Yours may be a little sweaty, I stored it in my back pocket.'

'Pocket? You were sporting speedos. Speedos don't have pockets,' I groaned.

'Ewwwww,' said Toe Jam with a smirk.

'Get over here and give me a hug you gnarly overgrown guinea pig.'

We had achieved our goals:

Mission: Doughnuts & Dungarees:
Check.

As for my young grasshopper? He took hold of a new level of maturity yesterday. This disciplemaking journey isn't always easy but it sure is worth every tube sock-wearing second!

So, journal, that's how the day rolled on.

Oh, I almost forgot. There was a knock at the door as we demolished our glazed blueberry fritters.

'I hear you had a splendid afternoon, full of incredible feats and unbelievable adventures!' she said, sounding strangely pleasant.

THE END

That wraps up Journal ENTRY #21.
So if you're reading these private notes in
my private journal about
my own disciplemaking journey...
Then Go Make Your Own
Dang Disciples!

THE HOSTS

I'm Bartus Mathetes

I was born to a pair of flute playing, nomadic grizzly wranglers. It was on one of their passes through the City of Giant Sleeping Croci with a band of Kodiaks that they came to understand the endless nature of the love of Christ in creation.

Phenominally Radnacious!

What can I say? They discipled me in the way, truth and life of Christ and here I am today. A college student with a receding hairline, a ratty old tie from an itinerant street preacher and a desire to make disciplemaking a way of life here in my town of WIDDLE WORTHINGTONVILLE.

I'm Toe Jam

Humans call me Toe Jam. I'm the seventh son of a fifth son of a cranky old barnstormer who was an only cub.

Before Bartus took me under his tutelage I was a tricycle-riding, cartwheel-slinging, leather chaps-wearing, hellion. Now, I still blaze trails on my tricycle while busting cartwheels in my chaps, but I'm taking on new traits as well. I'm discovering that I'm created in Christ with a purpose beyond my chaps. Love me some chaps!

THE AUTHOR

I'm R. J Dyson

That's right, I'm the husband of an incredibly wonderful wife and dad of 3 wildly awesome rapscallion disciples under my own roof. You won't believe it but I even went to kollege and studied the ancient Scriptures, like Bartus. Oh yeah, I'm also co-owner and creator at Absolutely Unprofessional.

Yep, that's a legitimate disciplemaking beard right there. It even helps with scribbling all the words and scratching all the pictures. And swimming, too.

Seriously. What's a disciple?

Like Bartus & Toe Jam discuseed around 5:03pm:
disciple = student.

Student of who? A **rabbi = teacher.** Jesus was a travelling rabbi who chose a bunch of unremarkable students to follow Him. A diverse group too! All ages and stages, eager to discover more about God and His plan for their lives and their tribe.

These students didn't *go* to school. They *lived* it!

Seriously, disciples in Jesus' day followed every footstep of their teacher. Studied the Bible with their rabbi. Learned how to start and end their days. Used the restroom when he did. Copied how he spoke to others and how he taught. They watched what he ate and who he spent time with. They learned it, lived it and passed it on.

It's a little different now so disciples and teachers are a little different too. All Christians are disciples of Jesus: his life and teachings. But we learn these best when we're being discipled by a mature Christian helping us connect the Gospel to our daily lives. A disciple who lives like Jesus. Like how Bartus has taken Toe Jam under his wing.

Go Read: *Matthew 28:16-20* See Jesus' simple plan for a worldwide disciplemaking movement. And He's still with us as the Ultimate Rabbi today.

Don't Let the Silliness Go to Waste!

Catch the Truth of Scripture lived out in the story and discuss it with your kids - your disciples:

Do you know that nearly any book, no matter how silly, serious or contentious, can be an opportunity for spiritual discussion and growth in Christ? Yes, that means even the crazy books your kids are reading might have some hidden value.

Including this one! It's true.

In fact, if you're looking for a way to redeem the silly adventure and immature comments of *Toe Jam*, then follow these itty-bitty instructions:

1. https://www.absolutelyunprofessional.com/creations

2. Click on Bartus & Toe Jam under *Books*.

3. Download the Disciple Q's Guide & get started! Who knows, there might even be some other things worth checking out.

www.ingramcontent.com/pod-product-compliance
Lightning Source LLC
Chambersburg PA
CBHW020330030826
48979CB00021B/513

* 9 7 8 0 9 9 1 4 5 8 1 8 9 *